I Still Hate to Read!

I Still Hate to Read!

written by

Rita Marshall

illustrated by

Etienne Delessert

Creative Editions

Mankato, Minnesota

. . . .

I'm a rebel.

I resist authority. I rob and plunder. I operate mysteriously
under several different identities. And only my dog Page
knows who I really am.

. . . .

My family sees only the Victor W. Dickens with freckles, two cowlicks, and size 8 1/2 shoes (the largest in my class!). The lousy student who hates to read, who can never find his homework in the dirty depths of his backpack. The B-minus daydreamer who's never on task.

My dad says I need to play sports—baseball, football, or some-
thing. He doesn't know that I took home the gold in the 1936
Olympics, running with Jesse Owens in the 400-meter relay.

. . . .

My mom insists I read books from the recommended lists at
the library. She doesn't know my secret library is online!

And then there's my little sister, Virginia. She has red hair and likes wearing velvet ribbons. She never daydreams. She recites poetry and looks up 5-syllable words in her dictionary. She plays hockey on the boys' team. She scores straight A's in school. And she is bossy.

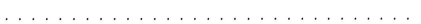

"Vic—tor, I'm going to tell if you don't

finish your chapter book!"

. . . .

When I was younger, I hated to read. But one night, I met a rabbit, a crocodile, a parrot, and a field mouse. We stayed up late traveling the world and becoming friends. Even now, I like to visit them whenever they can't sleep.

But as a rebel undercover—*I still hate to read.*

. . . .

Locked in my private chamber, I open a highly classified document and begin reading it to Page. We become a gang of ruthless outlaws roaming the Southwest Territory, stealing horses with Billy the Kid.

. . . .

Page and I have fought in the trenches during World War I.

We've suffered the Black Plague.

We've even tasted Japanese food.

*"Vic—tor, Dad says you have
to start your homework, NOW!"*

13

Sleuthing down dark, forsaken streets, we converse with rats and scavenge through litter, searching for the spirit of "The Black Cat," a one-eyed ghost named Pluto.

"Vic—tor, Mom says you have to let me in!"

We hitch a ride with a traveling circus. Page is a Bengal tiger.
She has an act with the white rabbit in black barn boots. I eat
fire, and the scrawny field mouse juggles chocolate coins.
The ringmaster is a raven with an emerald in his beak.

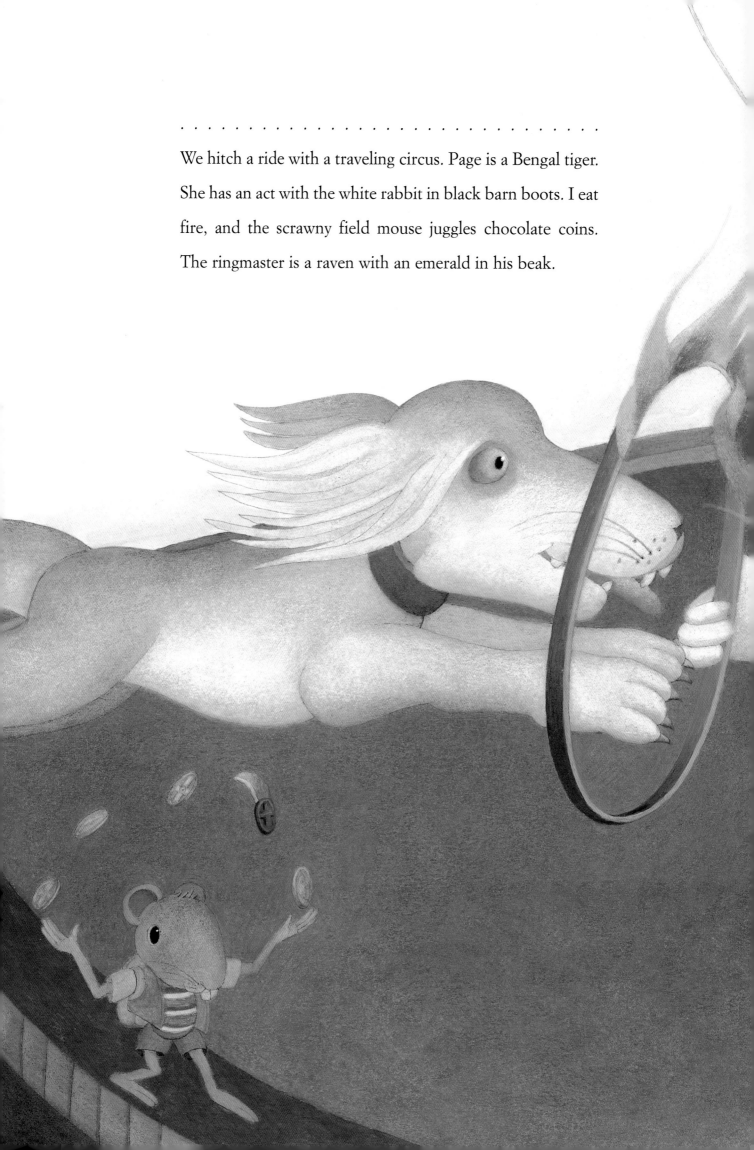

"Vic—tor, I'm telling! You're in there talking to yourself again!"

Virginia is the enemy queen set up to invade my castle with her armies of red ants. Page is my watchful knight. We remain silent until she retreats to her encampment. I immediately order that all insects be banished from the kingdom.

· ·

One day, Mrs. Willard, my fourth-grade teacher at Salisbury
Central School, asked everyone to bring a visual aid to the
next day's reading circle. A stuffed animal, a toy, or pictures
cut out of magazines, anything relating to a book about lions.

. . . .

After some careful thought, I decided upon a safari with my
pet lioness, Page. The plan was to cross the continent of
Africa, conquering and taming hordes of wild beasts—my
classmates.

Chaos reigned! "Only stuffed animals!" shouted Mrs. W. as Page lumbered into the room sniffing around. "No dogs allowed!" she barked.

Page drooled as she licked up a few stale cookie crumbs from the reading rug. Then she herded the students into a circle before settling down with a thud.

I opened the book and began to read. "She's listening!" observed Natalie Nickerson after a few sentences. "She's growing a mane!" exclaimed Ronnie Wilson, not knowing that only male lions grow manes. Page rolled over and gnawed on a few fleas.

Even kids who just hated to read quickly became members of her pride. Everyone took turns while the "queen of beasts" snored her way across the savanna. At story's end, the ruckus returned to the grasslands with the students growling, hissing, and roaring, "We love to read—to Page!"

. . . .

Days later, my parents received this note from Mrs. W.:

Dear Mr. and Mrs. Dickens,

Because your son and his lioness put on an A-plus per-formance for our reading enrichment circle this week, I'd like to assign them leading roles in the school musical, Every Dog Has His Day, *starring Hank the Cowdog. I certainly hope they will accept.*

Sincerely,

Mrs. E. Willard

"Mo—om, Victor's in his room again with the door locked!"

"Vir—gin—i—a, leave your poor brother alone and go practice your trumpet!"

I glanced at Page. Could I remain a rebel, now that I had allies in the house?

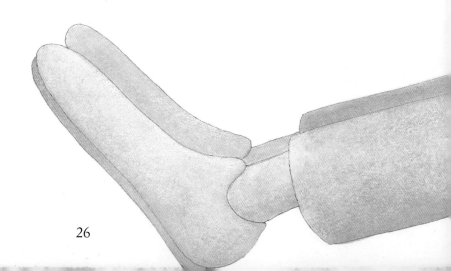

This was an unprecedented turn of events for a homeless writer living on the dank streets of Baltimore. My name was Poe. With emotion, I flung open "The Raven" and began to recite my darkest poem. Page cowered in the dim light. The wind howled.

> *...suddenly there came a tapping,*
> *As of someone gently rapping, rapping at*
> > *my chamber door.*
> *"'Tis some visiter," I muttered, "tapping at*
> > *my chamber door—*
> > *Only this and nothing more."*

Nothing more?—Nothing more than the allies and the ant queen at my chamber door.

"Is that Victor reading?" I heard my dad whisper.

"No, not Victor—he hates to read!" answered the ant queen with a smirk.

"Nevermore, Nevermore!" I crowed, wings flapping.

For Tom Peterson, who still hates to read.

Illustrations copyright © 2007 Etienne Delessert

Text copyright © 2007 Rita Marshall

Published in 2007 by Creative Editions

P.O. Box 227, Mankato, MN 56002 USA

Creative Editions is an imprint of The Creative Company.

Designed by Rita Marshall

Edited by Aaron Frisch

Printed in Italy

Library of Congress Cataloging-in-Publication Data

Marshall, Rita. I still hate to read! / by Rita Marshall;

illustrations by Etienne Delessert.

Summary: Now in fourth grade, Victor, the daydreamer

with a reputation as a bad student who hates to read,

secretly reads all the time.

ISBN: 978-1-56846-174-8

[1. Books and reading—Fiction. 2. Schools—Fiction.]

I. Delessert, Etienne, ill. II. Title.

PZ7.M356738Is 2007   [E]—dc22   2006030733

First edition

2 4 6 8 9 7 5 3 1